Mallory McDonald, Super Snoop

For my sisters, Leigh and Karen

♥ Laurie

For my sneaky little turkeys, Elliot and Juliette

—J.K.

Mallory McDonald, Super Snoop

by Laurie Friedman

illustrations by Jennifer Kalis

darby creek

MINNEAPOLIS

CONTENTS

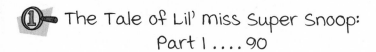
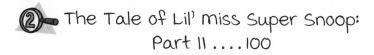

A WORD FROM MALLORY

This is Mallory McDonald, like the restaurant but no relation, age 10, reporting on location from 17 Wish Pond Road. If you don't know where that is, I'll tell you—it's my house. And if you don't know why I'm reporting the news, I'll tell you that too. It's because I have a lot of news to report.

The first item to report is that my mom and dad are going on vacation.

That's right. My parents, Harry and Sherry McDonald, claim they need a "getaway." So they're "getting away" for a week, and they say they're "looking forward" to it.

The next item worth reporting is that our babysitter,

Crystal, is coming to stay with my brother, Max, and me while our parents are gone.

The reason that's worth reporting is because Crystal is fun (well, more fun than my parents) so to be honest, I am "looking forward" to my parents' "getaway" as much as they are.

And in bigger news: Max has a girlfriend!

In case you missed it the first time, I'll repeat it: MAX HAS A GIRLFRIEND!

That's right! My brother, Max, and our next-door neighbor, Winnie, are boyfriend and girlfriend. Max says they are "official."

I'm not 100% sure what "official" means, but what I am sure about is that they are "officially" spending a lot of time together, and when they're together, they don't want me anywhere near them. I'm also not sure what they do when they're together, but I, Mallory McDonald, plan to find out.

I only have one thing to say on that topic: stay tuned!

DETECTIVES, INC.

"Brush your teeth," Mom says to Max and me.

"Don't worry!" my babysitter, Crystal, says for what I think is the fourth time but feels more like the four hundredth time. She gives Mom a *don't-worry-everything-will-be-fine-while-you're-gone* look.

But if you ask me, Mom still looks worried.

"Do your homework," she says. "And don't forget to floss and go to bed on time."

I think she's about to say something else, like *"eat your vegetables."* But Crystal interrupts her. "Don't worry, Mrs. McDonald. Everything will be fine." She guides my mom to the door like Mom is dropping off her child on the first day of kindergarten and it is time for her to go home.

Dad picks up the suitcases while Mom kisses Max and me good-bye for what I *know* is the four hundredth time.

Mom looks at Max and me. "I expect you two to treat each other extra nicely while we're gone." She says it like it's possible we would treat each other extra not-so-nicely just because they will be gone.

The truth is, we don't know how to treat each other when my parents are gone because they have never left us before. This is the first time my parents have ever gone away for a whole week, so I can see why Mom might be worried. But I don't think I'm the one she needs to worry about.

"You should be telling this to Max," I say to Mom. I make a face like I would never do anything wrong, especially while they are gone.

Max rolls his eyes.

Mom smiles. "Just be good to each other, and listen to Crystal."

"Don't worry!" Max and I say at the same time. Max and I almost never agree on anything, but I know neither one of us like long good-byes, especially when it involves my parents telling us all the things we should and shouldn't do while they are gone.

Dad waves and blows us both a kiss. Then he takes Mom's arm and they go.

"I'm out of here," Max says as soon as we hear their car roll away. He looks in the mirror over the table by the front door, combs his hair with his fingers, and then walks out.

"That was fast," says Crystal when the door slams shut.

I shrug like I'm used to that sort of thing. "Did you notice how he had to fix himself up before he left?" I ask Crystal.

She smiles. "Now that you mention it, I did. It was sort of an un-Max-like thing to do, wasn't it?"

"It was completely unlike the old Max but exactly like the new Max," I tell Crystal.

"This sounds interesting!" My babysitter wraps an arm around my shoulder. "Want to tell me more over a peanut butter and marshmallow sandwich?"

I nod and let Crystal steer me into the kitchen.

Crystal takes bread, peanut butter, and marshmallow creme out of a cabinet and starts assembling my favorite meal. "So what's going on?" she asks.

I make a drumroll sound like what I'm about to say is super important. "Max and Winnie are officially boyfriend and girlfriend."

I keep talking as Crystal puts a sandwich on a plate. "And ever since they became 'official,' they've officially been spending all of their time together."

Crystal nods like she's with me so far and wants to hear more, so I keep going.

"The thing is . . . when they're together, they never want me around. When I ask if I can hang out with them, they always say the same thing, which is 'NO!'"

Crystal slides my sandwich toward me like I should start eating. But I can't eat at a time like this. What I'm about to tell Crystal is V.I.I., which is short for *very important information.*

I ignore my favorite sandwich. "They're always together. They never include me in anything they do. I don't like it one bit. I live in this house too. Shouldn't I get to be part of what goes on here?"

I look at Crystal and wait for her to say something like, "Yes, Mallory. You have an absolute right to be part of whatever goes on in this house."

But that's not what she says. Crystal rubs her chin like she's choosing her words carefully.

"Mallory, Max has a right to spend time with Winnie." Crystal pauses. "And that means with Winnie alone." Crystal starts to explain something about him growing up and needing some privacy. But it sounds like blah, blah, blah to me.

While she is busy talking, my brain is busy thinking, and it thinks of an amazing idea. If I could pat myself on my own back for thinking of it, I would.

I interrupt Crystal's explanation.

"While you're here this week," I say, "why don't we band together like detectives? We can do a little spying and find out what Max and Winnie are up to when they're together."

Crystal shakes her head and takes a breath. "Mallory, did you hear anything that I just said? It is best to stay out of other people's business, no matter how interesting it might seem." She pauses like she's waiting for me to say something like I get it, but I don't.

Crystal keeps talking.

"Max and Winnie like each other and want to spend time together. What they do when they're together is their business, and you need to stay out of it."

"But I'm a kid," I say to Crystal. "Kids are naturally curious about interesting things, and to me, this is an interesting thing."

Crystal pats my head like she's sympathetic to the fact that I'm curious but that it still doesn't give me the right to spy. "Mallory, no detective work this week. And I mean it."

"But . . ." I start to explain to Crystal that as Max's younger sister, I just want to know what my older brother is up to, but Crystal stops me.

She raises my right hand and holds it up in the air. "Repeat after me," says Crystal. "I, Mallory McDonald, do solemnly swear to stay out of my brother's business."

I take a big bite out of my sandwich.

Everyone knows you can't solemnly swear anything when your mouth is full of peanut butter and marshmallow.

MALLORY ON A MISSION

It's Saturday afternoon, and I'm on a mission. A Mallory Mission. I just need one thing to make sure my mission is accomplished, and that one thing is named Mary Ann.

I walk next door to my best friend's house. If my babysitter won't help me, I know my best friend will.

I can already hear what she's going to

say when I ask her if she wants to help spy on my brother, Max, and her stepsister, Winnie.

"Count me in! I can't wait to find out what Max and Winnie are up to. Maybe we can dress up in disguises and follow them or plant listening devices and video cameras in their rooms. If Max picks his nose or Winnie says something weird, we'll know! This is going to be fun, fun, fun!"

Then she'll fall on the floor laughing and holding her sides, like just the idea of it sounds like fun.

I knock on the Winstons' door. Lucky for me, Mary Ann is the one who opens it.

"Just who I was looking for." I motion Mary Ann to follow me to her room. When we get there, I close the door. "I'm on a mission," I whisper. "And I need your help."

"Tell me more!" Mary Ann smiles like she's sure she's going to like what I have to say even though I haven't said it yet.

But as I explain that the mission I want her help with is figuring out what Max and Winnie do when they're together, which I remind Mary Ann is a lot of the time, Mary Ann's smile turns into a frown.

She starts to say something, but before the first word slips out of her mouth, I hold up my hand to stop her. Even though Mary Ann almost always wants to help me, I came prepared just in case she said no.

"I don't think you've thought about all the possible things Max and Winnie might be doing when they are alone together," I say to Mary Ann. "But I have." I stick my free hand in my back pocket, pull out a piece of paper, and start reading.

10 Things I, Mallory McDonald, Think Max and Winnie Might Be Doing When They Are Alone Together

Thing #1: Coming up with an evil plan to rule the world or, at the very least, Wish Pond Road.

Thing #2: Trying to turn themselves, or their younger siblings, into vampires. (I really hope this is not the case as I do not want to be a vampire.)

Thing #3: Trying to turn themselves, or their younger siblings, into werewolves. (I really, really hope this is not the case as I would rather be a vampire than a werewolf.)

Thing #4: Eating doughnuts. (Although Max probably has not shown Winnie that he can eat a dozen doughnuts in under a minute or they would not still be boyfriend and girlfriend.)

Thing #5: Writing love letters to each other.
   (I hope this is not what they are
   doing as Max is a terrible writer.)
Thing #6: Sitting quietly and reading a
   book. (If this is the case, I want
   to take a picture and send it to
   Grandma. She always says Max
   would benefit greatly from sitting
   quietly and reading a book.)
Thing #7: Taking each other's blood
   pressure. (I'm not quite sure what
   this is, but I hope they're not doing it.)
Thing #8: Thinking up ways to torture me.
   (I'm completely sure what this is, and
   I hope they're not doing it.)
Thing #9: Making plans to run away from
   home. (I'm also completely sure what
   this is, and I hope they are doing it.)
Thing #10: Staring into each other's
   eyes. (I've seen this in movies, and
   it's completely disgusting.)

When I finish reading, I wait for Mary Ann to say something like *"Count me in."* But she doesn't.

I wave my list in her face. "We have an awesome opportunity to find out which one of the things I just mentioned or any number of other things Max and Winnie might be doing."

But Mary Ann just shakes her head like none of the things on my list interest her in the least. "Sorry, Mallory. I promised C-Lo I would study for the spelling test with him."

My mouth opens so wide you could stick a dozen doughnuts in it and a vampire too.

"You'd rather study spelling than spy on Max and Winnie?"

Mary Ann grins. "The studying part doesn't sound like much fun, but doing it *with* C-Lo does."

I shake my head from side to side. I can't believe my best friend would rather study with her boyfriend than help me.

Mary Ann shrugs. "Spying on Max and Winnie doesn't sound so great anyway. As long as they're leaving us alone, who cares what they're doing?"

I kind of get that. Max is annoying, and Winnie isn't exactly what you'd call nice. "I'm glad they're leaving us alone," I say to Mary Ann. "But they've been spending all of their time alone, together. Aren't you a little curious about what they're up to?"

Mary Ann shakes her head like she's really not. "Sorry, Mallory. Maybe Joey will help you."

"Hmph." I can't believe Mary Ann won't help me. I walk down the hall to my other friend's room. When I tell Joey what I have in mind, I know he'll want to help.

But Joey is no more help than Mary Ann. "Mallory, why do you care what other people are doing?" He sounds like a parent or a teacher.

But since he's my age, I don't have to answer his question. I cross my arms across my chest and sit down quietly on his bed.

Joey sits down next to me. "I'm going to skateboard. Why don't you come with me?"

I shake my head. I'm on a mission, and skateboarding isn't part of it.

Joey bumps his shoulder into mine like he's being sensible and I'm not, and he's trying to bump some sense into me. "Mallory, why do you suddenly care what they're doing? You never cared before."

I can't believe I have to explain this to Joey. I take a deep breath. I try to make my voice sound patient while I explain to Joey what I think he should understand. "Whatever they were doing before, they weren't doing it together, and now they are. Don't you think that makes whatever it is they're doing much more interesting?"

Joey shrugs like that doesn't make it any more interesting at all. "Sorry, Mal."

I get up and start to walk out of his room.

"Mallory, forget about Max and Winnie," Joey says before I get to the door.

But I can't forget about Max and Winnie. In fact, I can't think about anything but Max and Winnie. It's like my brain is determined to find out what they're up to, and I can't stop it.

As I walk home, I think about Max and Winnie, and when I think about them, I think two things.

One. I'm *going* to find out what they're up to.

Two. I just need to figure out how to do it.

THREE'S A CROWD

"I'll be back in an hour," Max says to Crystal.

I crouch down behind the couch in the living room so Max can't see me. This isn't where I usually spend my Sunday mornings, but Max is in the kitchen telling Crystal where he is going and I need to hear every word he says.

I listen carefully.

I hear something about going with Winnie to take Champ on a walk and something important they need to talk about. I just can't hear what that something important is.

I stay in my hiding place and watch as Max takes a leash off the hook by the front door. I wait until I hear the front door slam.

Now is my chance.

I walk into the kitchen. "I'll be back in an hour," I say to Crystal.

She wrinkles up her nose like something smells funny. "Mallory, where are you going?"

I scoop up Cheeseburger and head for the front door. I grab a leash off the hook. "I'm going to take Cheeseburger on a walk," I say.

Crystal moves faster than a cheetah toward the front door, but I get there first. I'm determined to be part of the walking and talking that is going on this morning. "See you later," I wave and race out the door before Crystal has a chance to stop me.

When I get outside, Max and Winnie are already halfway down my street. I run to catch up with them. Now is my chance to find out what the important thing is that Max and Winnie need to talk about.

I catch up to my brother and Winnie and fall into place beside them as they walk.

Max looks at me like I have a bad case of chicken pox and he hasn't had the shot to keep him from getting it. "What are you doing?" asks Max.

I try to catch my breath. "I'm taking Cheeseburger for a walk." I set Cheeseburger down and hook the leash on to her collar.

"I've never heard of walking a cat," says Winnie.

I smile. "My cat likes to be walked."

Winnie blows a piece of hair out of her face. She gives Max a *this-is-ridiculous* look. "I've never seen you walk your cat before."

I smile. "She's in the mood to walk."

"Why don't you walk your cat another time." Max looks at me like that's something he'd really like me to do.

But I'd really like to do it now.

"Now is a good time," I say. I smile and start to walk, but Winnie doesn't budge. She puts her hand on her hip. "Max and I have something important we need to talk about." She says it as if whatever they have to talk about can't be talked about if I'm here.

I shrug. "You can talk in front of me. It won't bother me."

Winnie turns to Max and talks to him in a low voice like I can't hear what she's saying. But I can. "This is starting to annoy me," Winnie says.

Max gives me a look. I can tell he doesn't want Winnie to be annoyed. "Mallory, you can walk Cheeseburger another time."

I'm about to say, "I want to walk too." But Winnie crosses her arms and points to my house. I know she wants me to pick up my cat and go home, but that's not what I want to do.

I look at my brother. I give him my best *I'm-your-little-sister-and-I-just-want-to-walk-with-you* look. But I can tell it's not working. Max looks like he's about to explode.

Even though I really want to know what they're going to talk about, I really don't want my brother to explode. "It's a little hot out here for my cat," I say. I pick up Cheeseburger and walk back to the house.

"That was fast," Crystal says when I get inside.

I plop down on the couch. I tell Crystal that Max and Winnie wouldn't let me walk with them. "They never include me." I pout like it hurts that I'm not included, but the truth is, it mostly makes me mad.

"This was a perfect example of how they leave me out of everything they do," I say. "Now do you understand why I want to find out what they're up to?" I pause and wait for my babysitter to say she gets it, but she doesn't.

"Mallory, have you ever heard the expression 'three's a crowd?'"

She waits for me to answer.

I look down at the Band-Aid on my knee. My third-grade teacher, Mrs. Daily, taught us all kinds of sayings, and that was one of them.

"Of course, I've heard that expression," I tell Crystal. "But I don't like it. Max is my brother, and as his sister, I should get to know what he's talking about when he says he has something 'important' he needs to talk about. What if he's in trouble? Maybe I could help."

"Mal, I don't think Max is in trouble. I just think he wants some privacy." My babysitter points to the crystal ball she always brings to my house when she babysits.

"Let's see what the ball has to say." She rubs her crystal ball and looks into the glass.

Then she wraps an arm around me. "The ball says you will

This ball needs to go back to Crystal Ball School.

be just fine if you take care of your own business and stay out of your brother's."

Crystal smiles like she's certain the ball knows what it's talking about.

Here's what I'm certain about: I want to know what my brother and his girlfriend are talking about. And somehow, some way, I'm going to find out.

READING TIME

I look at my watch, and it tells me what I already knew . . . my brother has been on the computer for a very long time.

And it doesn't take a genius to know who he's talking to on it.

I walk over to the desk and tap my brother on the shoulder. "Max, it's my turn," I say. But he ignores me.

I give his shoulder a little *time-to-get-up* shove. But Max doesn't budge.

"C'mon," I say. "You've been there for so long, your butt has probably glued itself to the chair." But Max doesn't seem like that possibility concerns him in the least.

Portrait of a boy who doesn't care that he's glued to a chair.

I look at my babysitter like I could use some help, but Crystal is busy washing the dinner dishes.

I walk across the kitchen and tap her on the shoulder. Then I point to where Max is sitting. "Crystal, Max has been on there all night."

I wait for her to say, *"Max, get off the computer and give your sister a turn."* But that's not what she says.

"Mallory. Max. Remember what your mom said about doing your homework?" Crystal puts her dish towel down on the counter. "It's Sunday night, and I want you two to start the week off right. It's reading time."

Max groans like the last thing he wants to do on Sunday night is read. He picks up his social studies book off the counter. "I'm going to my room," he says.

Crystal nods. She seems happy that Max is cooperating. Then she looks at me. I guess it is my turn to cooperate too.

I nod like I plan to be cooperative. And I do plan to be cooperative. Fully cooperative. Crystal's idea gives me a great idea of my own.

I grab my science book and follow my brother out of the kitchen. "I'm going to my room too," I say to Crystal.

She looks happy to see that both McDonald children are cooperating.

"See you later," I say as I walk out of the kitchen. I smile as I walk to my room. Crystal said we have to read, but she didn't say *what* we have to read.

When I get to my room, I sit down on my bed next to Cheeseburger. "Good news," I tell my cat. "As soon as Crystal is done in the kitchen, we're going back in."

Cheeseburger purrs, but then she tilts her head to the side like she wants me to explain why we're going.

"It's simple," I whisper. "Max always forgets to log off the computer. All we have to do is wait until we hear Crystal's footsteps on the stairs. Then we can go see what Max wrote."

I lie back against my pillows, put my hands behind my head, and cross my feet.

I feel like a detective who is about to wrap up a case. The mystery of what Max is up to is about to be solved.

I pick up my science book and try to start reading while I'm waiting, but the truth is, I'm too excited to read.

I look at my watch and decide to count the number of times the second hand passes the 12 until I hear footsteps on the stairs. One. Two. Three. Four. Five. I keep counting. Six. Seven. Eight. Nine. Ten. No footsteps. Eleven. Twelve. Thirteen. Fourteen. Still no footsteps. I don't know what is taking Crystal so long. I try to take a deep breath and relax, but I feel like I'm about to pop. Fifteen. Sixteen. Seventeen. Footsteps, finally!

That was the slowest seventeen minutes in history. I stand up and gently scoop up my cat. "Time to go," I whisper to Cheeseburger in my quietest voice.

Even though Crystal is in my parent's room and Max is in his room, if I'm going to do this, I'm going to have to do it without making a sound.

I tiptoe down the hall.

When I get to the kitchen, I put Cheeseburger down slowly and put my finger to my lips to tell her to be quiet too. Then I sit down carefully in the chair as though I'm sitting on a chair made out of eggshells and I don't want to break it.

I press on the keyboard with one finger as gently as I can. It makes a little clicking noise, but hopefully nobody heard it.

I look at the screen. Max's e-mail inbox is still up. As Mary Ann would say, "WOW! WOW! WOW!" I feel like I just hit the jackpot.

Max has forty-seven saved e-mails in his inbox. I scroll down the list. They're all from one person, and that one person's e-mail name is glamgirl. Just who I thought would be writing my brother.

Even though I'm super happy that my hunch was right and I'm about to find out what my brother is up to, I'm a little nervous too.

Part of me knows I shouldn't be reading Max's e-mail, but more of me wants to know what my brother is doing.

I think about how curious I've been to know what my brother is doing.

I think what could happen to me if I don't find out.

I have to know. I take a deep breath and click on the first e-mail.

SUBJECT: What we were talking about earlier

FROM: glamgirl

TO: sportzdude

Max,

I love our plan!

See you tomorrow after school and we'll get started.

Your room is a good place to do it.

XOXO, Winnie

When I'm done reading the e-mail, I gasp. What in the world are my brother and Winnie going to do in his room after school tomorrow? It could be anything. I have to find out! I click on the next e-mail. But when I do, I feel a hand on my shoulder.

"Mallory! What are you doing?"

I jump. "You scared me!" I say to Crystal.

She ignores my jumpiness and looks over my shoulder at the computer screen. Then she crosses her arms across her chest. "Mallory, why are you reading your brother's e-mails?"

"I . . . um . . ." I try to find the right words to explain why I was reading Max's e-mails, but my mouth seems to not be working properly. I point to the screen like Crystal should see for herself that Max and Winnie are planning to do something tomorrow after school in his room.

But Crystal shakes her head like she has no interest in reading what's on the screen.

Her only interest seems to be in what I was doing reading it.

"Mallory, you absolutely *cannot* read other people's e-mails! You were supposed to be in your room reading your schoolwork."

Crystal does not look happy. She pulls on my arm to get me up from the chair. She points to my room. "March, young lady!"

I don't even look at Crystal as I walk to my room. I know she doesn't understand why I would want to read my brother's e-mails. The truth is, I wouldn't have to read my brother's e-mails if he would just tell me what he's up to, but he won't.

I know he and Winnie are planning to do something. I know *where*: in his room. I know *when*: after school tomorrow. The only thing I don't know is *what*.

I walk in my room and shut the door.

I, Mallory McDonald, am going to figure it out.

A WEEK IN REVIEW

Question: What does Friday afternoon have in common with Sunday night?

My answer: everything.

If you're wondering what I mean by that, I'll tell you.

On Sunday night, I read Winnie's email to Max that said they were going to do something in his room.

I spent all week trying to figure out what that something was. It is now Friday afternoon, and I still don't know exactly what it is they have been doing all week in his room.

I know what they told Crystal they were doing. I know what Crystal says they were doing. But I didn't see them doing it.

Here's what happened.

MONDAY

On Monday after school, I tried to answer the *what-are-Max-and-Winnie-doing-in-his-room?* question by knocking on his door and asking them that question.

But when I asked, Max's answer was, "Get lost!"

If you ask me, that was not really an answer. So I knocked again. This time, Max opened the door and said they were working on their science fair project and didn't have time for any more interruptions. Then he closed the door again.

If you ask me, that was still not really an answer. The reason I don't think that was an answer was because when Max opened his door, which I will admit was kind of quickly, I didn't see anything like strange plants or smell anything like stinky chemicals that would make me believe they were actually working on a science fair project.

I thought maybe I could bribe them. So after a trip to the kitchen, I knocked on Max's door a third time.

This time when I knocked, I said, "I have cookies." The good news is that when I said that, Winnie opened the door. The bad news is that she took the plate in my hand and shut the door just as fast as she opened it.

That was when I told Crystal that Max and Winnie *say* they are working on a science fair project in his room but that I don't have any *proof* that that is what they are doing.

Crystal said she had all the proof she needed that they were doing what they said they were doing because she checked on them and, when she did, that was exactly what they were doing.

Then she said the only other proof she needed was proof that I was doing my own work. She escorted me to my room, closed the door, and said she would be back in a little while to check. Then she said something else about me needing to spend the rest of the afternoon doing my work and not worrying about what my brother was doing.

So that is what I did and not because I wanted to but because that is what somebody (named Crystal) made me do.

TUESDAY

On Tuesday after school, Max and Winnie were right back in his room, right where they had been the day before. Even though Crystal said Max and Winnie were still working on a science fair project, I wasn't so sure that was exactly what they were doing.

The reason I wasn't sure is because when I asked if I could see their project, they said, "NO."

That made no sense to me. They said they were working on a *science* project, not a *secret* project. So I decided to find out just what they were doing in his room.

Here's what happened: I put on black leggings and a long-sleeved black T-shirt. I put on black socks and shoes and gloves and a hat. I put on dark sunglasses. Then I got out my magnifying glass and tape recorder.

When I looked in the mirror, I thought I looked exactly like a P.I. (which, if you don't know, is short for *private investigator*).

I was ready to uncover the mystery of what Max and Winnie were doing in his room.

I crawled down the hall like a cat. When

I got to Max's door, I positioned myself on the floor outside his door. I turned on my tape recorder. I tried to look under the door. Just when I located two pairs of feet, I felt a hand around my ankle.

It will probably not surprise you to hear that the hand belonged to Crystal. She took my tape recorder and walked me back to my room, where she played a little game she called Babysitter Charades. It went like this.

"Four words." Crystal held up a finger. "First Word. *Leave.*" She held up two fingers. "Second word. *Your.*" She held up another finger. "Third word. *Brother.*" She held up a fourth finger. "Fourth word. *Alone.*"

It didn't take a genius to put those four words together.

Also, no genius required to know those were not the four words I wanted to hear.

WEDNESDAY

The next day after school, Max and Winnie were right back where they were the day before and the day before that. In Max's room with the door closed!

When I asked why they were spending so much time in his room, Max said, "Which part of 'we are working on our science fair project' is hard for you to understand?"

The answer to that question (which I did not say out loud) was that none of it was hard for me to understand. I just didn't believe it. I mean, how long can a science fair project take? I am no science fair project expert, but I don't see how it could take three days.

So I decided to look and see if a science fair project can take three days.

I went online and typed in: *How long can a Science Fair project take?*

I pressed enter and waited for my answer. The answer the computer gave me was that some projects can take weeks or even months.

So I clicked off the computer. Everybody knows you can't believe everything you read on the Internet anyway. I knew something funny was going on in Max's room, and I was determined to find out what that something was.

I tried to explain it to Crystal so she would understand. I told her I had my doubts that science was really what Max and Winnie were doing back there, but if they were, it could be dangerous science, like creating explosives or making poisonous chemicals, and that as the babysitter in charge this week, she needed to check it out.

When I said that, Crystal laughed and said she had already checked, several times, and that I didn't need to worry.

But I told her someone needs to worry. I reminded her that there are a lot of people and animals in this house and that she's supposed to be the one in charge of keeping them safe!

Then she laughed even harder and said something about me being very creative.

To be honest, I do not think she meant it as a compliment.

THURSDAY

As you can see, I hadn't had much luck in figuring out what Max and Winnie were up to. So on Thursday, I decided to ask the smartest person I know for some help.

That person is my friend, Pamela.

When I told her what was going on, she told me that she had a feeling Max and Winnie were actually working on a science fair project because she knew the sixth grade was having a science fair.

What Pamela didn't know is that my brother has never worked on any kind of project for more than a few minutes, so it didn't make much sense that he was working on this project for a few days.

When I told Pamela that, she said she is pretty smart about school projects, but doesn't know much about older brothers. She said the only thing she knows about them, and she said she only knows this from books she's read, is that it is generally best to leave them alone when they don't want to be bothered.

Then she said that if I needed to know more than that, the person I should ask is Helpful Hannah.

I slapped my head when she said that. I don't know why I hadn't thought of it before. Everybody knows Helpful Hannah is the most helpful advice columnist on the Internet and that if it's help you need, Hannah is the one to go to.

When I got home from school, I sat right down at the computer and started my letter.

Subject: My brother and his girlfriend
From: malgal
To: Helpful Hannah

Dear Hannah,
I am a ten-year-old girl with a problem. My older brother has a girlfriend, and

they don't want me anywhere near them. They have what you might call a "closed door" policy, which means they have been spending a lot of time in his room lately with his door closed. They say they are working on a science fair project. My babysitter says the same thing. But here's what I'm saying: This is rude! Rude! Rude! Rude! He should open his door and let me in. Don't you agree? I'm sure you do. Also, don't you agree that since my brother is my brother and we live in the same house, he should have to include me in what he's doing if I want to be included? Thanks. I knew you would agree with everything I am thinking. Just writing to you makes me realize that I am not the one with the problem. It's my brother who needs help. When you write back, you do not need to address your letter to me. You can address it to my brother (his name is Max). Just tell him to open his door and let me in.

Thanks again. Problem solved.

Signed,

Little Sister Without a Problem

When I was done typing, I clicked off the computer and ate a banana. All I had to do was wait for Helpful Hannah to help.

FRIDAY

It's Friday afternoon. Max and Winnie are still in his room. I still haven't figured out what they're doing in there. And I still haven't heard from Hannah.

When I was in third grade, my teacher Mrs. Daily taught us the expression "when opportunity knocks." She said it means when an opportunity comes along, you shouldn't let it pass you by. As far as I'm concerned, opportunity has not knocked this week.

Everything I have tried has failed. But I'm not going to fail again.

I'm going to solve this mystery.

I go into the kitchen and take a good look around. Then, I take out a notepad, some pencils, a bag of M&Ms, and some cat treats. I take a deep breath.

I have everything I need to solve this mystery.

Well, I have everything I need to *think* of a way to solve this mystery . . . which is exactly what I'm going to do now.

A GIRL WITH A PLAN

I lay my notepad, pencils, M&Ms, and cat treats out on the bed beside me.

Then I call this bedroom meeting to order.

"All in favor of coming up with a plan to find out what Max and Winnie are doing when they're alone together, raise your right hand."

Since I'm the only one at this meeting with a hand, I raise mine. I reach over and grab Cheeseburger's paw and hold it up in the air. If no one else will help me, at least I can count on my cat.

"Time to brainstorm," I tell Cheeseburger. I open up the M&Ms and pop a few in my mouth. Then I give Cheeseburger a cat treat. "We need brain food if we're going to brainstorm," I tell my cat. She purrs like she agrees.

"OK," I say out loud. "We need to come up with a plan to find out what Winnie and Max are up to. Any ideas?"

Cheeseburger curls up beside me and closes her eyes.

I pop another M&M into my mouth. I think about all the things I've done that haven't worked.

I've tried getting my babysitter and my friends to help me spy.

I've tried reading Max's emails.

I've tried eavesdropping outside his door.

I've gone online and done research.

I've even asked an expert.

Nothing I've tried has worked at all.

I shake Cheeseburger to wake her up, and I give her a cat treat. "Cheeseburger, I could use some help here."

She stretches and sniffs the bag of cat treats.

I open up a notebook and start making notes.

"We could feed Max and Winnie truth serum so they would have to tell us what they're doing," I say out loud.

I wait to see if Cheeseburger responds, but she just keeps sniffing.

I make some more notes.

"Install a video camera in Max's room so I could see what they're doing."

"Send an official-looking letter that looks like it's from a lawyer that says they have to tell me what they're doing or risk going to jail."

I look at my notes. Then I rip that sheet of paper out of the notebook. I crumple it up into a ball and throw it across my room toward the garbage can.

It misses and lands on the floor.

Urrrgh. It's so frustrating to want to think of something and to not be able to. I have to think of something.

I scratch my head.

I eat more M&Ms.

I cross my toes.

I close my eyes to try to help myself think. I do what Grandma does when she's doing yoga. I sit crossed-legged. I take three deep breaths. In through my nose. Out through my mouth.

But it doesn't help. Nothing is helping.

I open my eyes and reach over to pet Cheeseburger, but when I do, Cheeseburger is gone and so is the bag of cat treats.

"Cheeseburger!" I say her name loudly like I want her to come out now, but she doesn't respond. I say her name again, but no sign of Cheeseburger.

I look under my bed and behind my desk. Still no sign of Cheeseburger.

I can't believe it . . . my cat is hiding from me. "CHEESEBURGER!" I say in my *come-out-now* voice.

But that cat does not come out.

I need to be thinking right now, not looking for a cat.

I look in the bathroom and next to the pile of wet towels on the floor. Still no sign of Cheeseburger.

I go back in my room and look around. The only other place Cheeseburger could be is in my closet. When I look, I find her and her bag of cat treats on top of my shoes and a pile of dirty clothes.

I scoop her up and shake my head. "Cheeseburger, why would you hide in the closet when you're supposed to be helping me brainstorm?"

Cheeseburger makes a noise, like she's trying to tell me something.

I look at her and think for a minute. Then I sit down on my bed. I slap my head. I can't believe I didn't think of it myself.

Hide-and-seek. It's the perfect plan!

I pat Cheeseburger on the head. "You're a genius," I say to my cat. "A little game of Hide-and-seek will tell me exactly what I need to know."

World's Smartest Cat!!

I look at the clock. Then I make another note in my notebook.

As the saying goes, "Let the games begin." And they will. Right after dinner.

HIDE-AND-SEEK

"Who wants the last slice?" Crystal holds up an extra-large pizza box.

Mary Ann shakes her head. "I'm stuffed."

Winnie groans like she ate too much too.

Even Joey and Max say they don't want any more.

"Mallory, this piece has your name on it," says Crystal.

"No thanks," I tell my babysitter. Pizza is not what I want right now. What I want is to play a game, and that game is called hide-and-seek.

I feel like eating pizza has never taken so long.

I count to ten in my head and wait for my babysitter to say what she says every Friday night when we're done with dinner.

"So what do you peeps want to do next?" Crystal asks, just like I knew she would.

But before Joey has time to say *"skateboard"* or Mary Ann has time to say *"watch a movie"* or Max and Winnie have time to disappear, I seize the moment I've been waiting for.

"Let's play hide-and-seek!" I clap my hands together like I'm really excited about the idea, and the truth is, I am really excited about the idea. While I was eating pizza, I couldn't stop thinking about how good my plan is.

"That sounds like fun," says Mary Ann.
Crystal nods like she likes my idea too.
"I'm in," says Joey.

Max shakes his head like he's not.
"That's a game for babies." He looks at
Winnie like he's speaking for both of them.
"We don't want to play," he says.

I knew my brother wouldn't say yes right away, but I'm prepared. I cross my toes and hope that what I'm about to say next works.

"Please, Max." I wring my hands together and give my brother and his girlfriend my best *it-would-make-me-really-happy-if-the-two-of-you-said-yes* face. "You and Winnie can be 'it' together, and everyone else will hide."

Max shakes his head like even the idea of being "it" with Winnie isn't enough to make him want to play. But lucky for me, someone does like that idea.

"I think it sounds like fun," says Winnie.

When Winnie says that, Max agrees to play right away. I uncross my toes. My plan is working just like I hoped it would.

"OK. You and Winnie count to one hundred, and we'll all hide."

...five ...Six... ...seven...

Winnie and Max close their eyes and start counting. One, two, three, four . . . I point Joey and Crystal to the kitchen and laundry room and Mary Ann to my room.

Max and Winnie keep counting. Sixteen, seventeen, eighteen . . . Everyone goes off to hide in the direction I point them to like I'm the one in charge.

If I had time to pat myself on the back for my plan going even better than I'd hoped, I would, but I don't. Max and Winnie are counting fast. Thirty-two, thirty-three, thirty-four . . .

I don't have much time.

I tiptoe down the hall to Max's room. I know exactly where I'm going to hide. Fifty-one, fifty-two, fifty-three . . .

I quietly open the door to Max's closet. Sixty-seven, sixty-eight, sixty-nine . . .

I lie down on the floor on top of Max's shoes. It isn't the most comfortable place to hide. Seventy-nine, eighty, eighty-one . . .

I grab a pile of Max's dirty clothes from the extra-large pile of dirty clothes on the floor of his closet.

I start covering myself up with shorts, shirts, socks, and baseball pants. Eighty-seven, eighty-eight, eighty-nine . . . This also isn't the best-smelling hiding place. Ninety-one, ninety-two, ninety-three . . .

I'm running out of time. I keep covering myself until I'm completely covered in smelly, dirty clothes. Ninety-seven, ninety-eight, ninety-nine . . . I'm so covered in dirty clothes, I can barely breathe. I leave a tiny crack open so I can see.

"One hundred. Here we come!"

My heart is racing. I hope my hiding place is as good as I think it is. I hope I find out what I'm trying to find out.

I hear footsteps going up the stairs.

"I don't see anyone up here," I hear Winnie say to Max.

More footsteps. This time they sound like they're coming from the hall. I can hear them getting closer. Winnie and Max are coming my way.

I can see them as they walk into Max's room.

"Do you think there's anyone in here?" Winnie asks.

Max looks under the bed and under the desk. He opens the closet door. I try not to breathe or make a sound. "There's nothing in here but a bunch of dirty clothes."

Winnie sits down on Max's bed and eyes the pile in his closet. "You should do some laundry." She makes a face like the size of the pile in Max's closet is disgusting.

Max shrugs like the pile in the closet doesn't bother him. He sits down on the bed beside Winnie. "This game is boring," he says.

Max has a nervous look on his face. What's weird is that my brother never looks nervous.

Something tells me this might be the moment I've been waiting for. I think I'm about to find out what they've been doing back here all week. And I don't think it's just a science fair project.

"So what do you want to do?" asks Winnie.

Max moves a little closer to Winnie. She sits very still like she's waiting, just like I am, for something to happen.

Max just sits there.

Winnie looks at him. "We should either do something or play the game."

Max looks like he's about to throw up. It kind of makes me want to laugh, but I bite my lip. Now would not be a good time to laugh.

Winnie shrugs like Max's opportunity to do something other than play hide-and-seek

is over. She starts to stand up, but Max stops her.

I've never seen my brother look so nervous. "I'd like to do this," Max says. Then he leans over and kisses Winnie on the cheek.

I blink. It was such a quick kiss that part of me isn't even sure I saw it.

But I did. My brother just kissed a girl, and I saw it.

I can't believe it! My plan worked. The mystery of what Max and Winnie do when they are alone together is officially solved. I can't believe I got to the bottom of this. I can't wait to tell Mary Ann and Joey and even Crystal.

They will finally understand why I've been so curious about what Max and Winnie do when they are together. I knew it wasn't just science.

I can't wait to tell everyone what I saw. There's only one thing stopping me, and that thing is a big pile of dirty, smelly clothes.

THE TALE OF LIL' MISS SUPER SNOOP: PART I

By Mallory McDonald

Once upon a time there was a curious, adorable, extremely creative girl with red hair and freckles who solved the mystery of what her big brother and his girlfriend were doing when they were alone. She did this seemingly difficult task by simply hiding under a pile of dirty clothes.

This was a mystery that had been very puzzling to the girl for a while, and she was very happy when she solved it.

She was so happy when she solved it that she decided to tell other people (which included her best friends and her babysitter) about what she saw when she was hiding under the pile of dirty clothes.

At first, she thought what she saw (which was her brother kissing his girlfriend while they were supposed to be playing hide-and-seek) was very interesting.

But as she thought about it a little more, she decided it wasn't quite as interesting as she had initially thought it was. In fact, when she thought back over what she saw, she thought in her mind that it happened kind of quickly and not in a very exciting way. And as she continued to think about it, she decided that what she saw wasn't nearly as interesting as she thought it could have been.

So, she did what extremely creative people often do (remember, earlier in the story, we said she was extremely creative) when things aren't all that interesting. They make them seem more interesting.

Hmmm... This could be more interesting...

This is exactly what the girl did for her best friends and her babysitter.

When she told them what she saw while she was hiding under the pile of dirty clothes, she used her creative skills to make the story of her brother kissing his girlfriend sound as interesting as she could possibly make it.

The first people she told were her best friends.

When she told them that she saw her brother kiss his girlfriend, she did not tell them that the kiss was small and quick and on the cheek. To the contrary, she described it as long and slow and definitely not on the cheek.

She told them that it was the kind of kiss you might see on TV or even in the movies. When she told her friends that, they seemed to be very interested in the way she was describing what she saw, so she kept creatively describing what she saw.

She told her friends that the kiss that she saw was not just the kind you see on regular TV or in plain old movies, but more like the kind you see in romantic movies.

The Academy Award for Best Kiss goes to...

When she told her friends that, they were amazed. And this made the girl very happy.

Even though her friends had told her

they did not think what her brother and their stepsister were doing together was all that interesting, and one of her friends had even told her that she should stay out of their business, when she told them what she saw, they were both very interested. In fact, they wanted to know more.

So she told them more. She used her most extreme creativity (remember, we said she was extremely creative) to think of some more things to tell them.

She told them that all week, her brother and his girlfriend had been in his room with the door closed. She told them that all week they said they were working on a science fair project, but she didn't think that was the case because all week she had heard laughter coming out of her brother's room. She also told them that she had heard noises that sounded like kissing noises. She said when she first heard the noises, she thought maybe there was something wrong with Max's dog, Champ, but then she realized what it was.

When she said that, her two best friends laughed like crazy. They laughed so loud and so hard that the girl's babysitter came into the room to ask what was so funny.

So . . . thinking that her babysitter was fun (at least, more fun than her parents), the curious, adorable, extremely creative girl told her babysitter the same story she told her friends. Only this time, she added in even more extremely creative details.

The Kiss, as Overheard by Miss Mallory McDonald

Winnie, I love you, darling.

Smooch Smooch

You're my prince, Max!

Max's Room KEEP OUT!

And when she finished telling this incredibly creative account of what happened in her brother's room while she was hiding under a pile of dirty laundry, she waited. She waited for her babysitter to laugh loud and hard just like her friends did.

But much to this poor girl's dismay, that is not what happened.

Unfortunately, that is not what happened at all.

The girl's babysitter did NOT laugh. She did the opposite of laughing. She got mad. VERY, VERY MAD.

She started to talk to the girl in a very mad kind of way.

FOR SALE:
One mad babysitter

She said she couldn't believe that the girl had hidden in her brother's room and spied on him AFTER she had told the girl NUMEROUS times to stay out of her brother's business.

She said she couldn't believe the girl was telling other people what she had seen.

She even suggested that maybe what the girl said she had seen might not be what actually happened.

Then she said she was going to get to the bottom of this, and she told the girl to sit down on the couch and not to move, that this meeting was T.B.C.

Which if you don't know, is babysitter talk for "to be continued."

THE TALE OF LIL' MISS SUPER SNOOP: PART II

By Mallory McDonald

So the tale of Lil' Miss Super Snoop continued.

It continued when, much to the girl's extreme dismay, her babysitter returned. But she didn't return alone.

She returned with the girl's brother and his girlfriend.

And to be honest, they (the brother and the girlfriend) looked just as mad as the babysitter had looked before she went to get them.

Then the babysitter told everyone to sit down. But the brother did not sit down.

The girl tried to say to the babysitter that her brother was not doing as the babysitter said (which was to sit down), but the babysitter told the girl to be quiet. She said she would let her know when it was her turn to talk.

Even though she did not tell the girl's brother that it was his turn to talk, he seemed to think that it was, and the babysitter did not seem to mind.

The brother talked a lot. And so did his girlfriend.

They said they were really mad at the girl.

The brother said that the babysitter told him that she hid in his room and that he was FURIOUS!!!

The girl reminded her brother that the reason she was hiding was because they were playing hide-and-seek, and that is what you are supposed to do.

But this made the girl's brother even more FURIOUS!!!

And it made the girlfriend pretty mad too.

Both of them started ranting and raving (which means yelling like crazy people) that the girl had made up all kinds of things that just weren't true.

Then they started saying what some of the things were that she had said.

Is this a couple you would want to spend time with?

When they started saying these things, the girl looked at the babysitter and said what any girl would say in her position. She said to the babysitter, "Why did you tell them what I said?"

Unfortunately for the girl, this seemed to be exactly the wrong thing to say.

When she said this, it made her brother and his girlfriend even more FURIOUS!!! It was like they weren't 100% sure before if she had actually said those things. But now, they knew that she had.

That was when the brother and his girlfriend came completely unglued.

They were yelling all kinds of things about what the girl had said and done. They yelled loudly and for a long time. They yelled that the girl should mind her own business. They yelled and yelled and yelled. And just when it seemed like

they couldn't possibly find anything else to yell about, the girl's brother told her that she was a snoop with a big mouth. In fact, he said these exact words to her: "ARE YOU HAPPY NOW, LIL' MISS SUPER SNOOP?"

The girl was not happy.

She didn't like being yelled at, and she didn't like being called names either.

The girl reminded the babysitter that saying she was a super snoop was name-calling and that her parents do not allow name-calling in their home.

Unfortunately for the girl, the babysitter seemed to ignore this information. She just looked at the girl (and not in a very nice way) and said, "You owe your brother and Winnie an apology."

So the girl apologized.

But the girl's brother and his girlfriend didn't seem like they accepted her apology. So the girl started to talk.

If you remember earlier in the story, the babysitter had said she would let the girl know when it was her time to talk, and it seemed like now was her time.

But when she started to talk, the babysitter stopped her. She told the girl to save her explanation about why she did what she did.

Then the babysitter said something that the girl did not like hearing at all.

She said, "Wait until your parents get home."

The reason the girl did not like hearing that was because her parents were coming home that night.

And she knew they would not be happy. Poor girl.

WISHFUL
THINKING

One of the expressions Mrs. Daily taught our class last year was *"too little, too late."*

She said it means that something that is supposed to be helpful is not helpful enough and arrives too late to save the situation. That is exactly the kind of help that I got from Helpful Hannah.

When I apologized to Max and Winnie, they did not accept my apology, so I went on the computer to write Helpful Hannah for some more help.

But when I did, I saw that she had written back to me to answer the last time I had written to her. I clicked on her email.

Subject: Here's a little help
From: Helpful Hannah
To: Malgal

Dear Malgal,

I got your letter, and I have some very simple advice for you. (I will write your brother if he writes to me, but to be honest, it does not seem like he needs advice.) Here it is: The best way to get your brother to include you is just to stay out of his business. No peeking. No sneaking. No snooping. I am quite sure if you do this, in time, he will want to spend more time with you and start to include you in some of his activities.

I hope this helps.

Helpfully yours,

Hannah

I click off the computer. Hannah's advice wasn't too helpful. Maybe it would have been if I had gotten it yesterday, but I didn't.

I wonder if Hannah knows what to do when your parents come home from a trip and they are mad. She might, but unfortunately for me I don't have time to find out.

My parents will be home any minute, and I know they won't be happy when they get here.

I walk outside and down to the wish pond. When I get there, I pick up a rock, squeeze my eyes shut, and make a wish.

I wish my parents won't come home.

But I don't throw my rock into the wish pond. I really do want my parents to come home. I just don't want them to be mad at me when they arrive.

I close my eyes again and remake my wish.

I wish my parents won't be mad at me when they get home.

I throw my rock and watch as it sinks into the wish pond. Unfortunately, I think my wish is wishful thinking. I heard Crystal on the phone telling my parents what happened.

They will be home any minute, and something tells me that even though I made a big sign that says, *"Welcome home, Mom and Dad!"* their homecoming is not going to be a happy one.

I scoop up Cheeseburger and give her a hug.

I really don't want to face Mom and Dad. Max and Winnie and Crystal have already gotten mad at me, and I am not looking forward to dealing with more people who are mad.

I am also not looking forward to explaining to Mom and Dad why I did what

I did. I know they are going to ask. But I don't know what I am going to say.

I take a deep breath and start walking home from the wish pond. Who knows, maybe I will get lucky and my parents will be in a *free pass* mood. Maybe they had such a good time on vacation that they'll be too happy to be mad.

I guess I'll have to wait and see what happens when they get here.

Things I would like to see:
- A good movie
- A $100 bill on the ground
- My room magically cleaned up
- Happy Parents

Things I don't want to see:

Mad Parents

But I don't have to wait long. My parents' blue van turns on to my street. When they pass me, Dad stops and rolls down his window. "Mallory, please get in the van."

I look at Dad's face as I get in. He does not look happy. I wait for him to say something like, *"Hello. How are you? Sweet Potato, we sure missed you."* But Dad doesn't say anything like that. It doesn't take a genius to know this is not a good start.

The second I sit down, both of my parents turn around and look at me. I smile like I'm happy to see them, but I'm the only person smiling in this van. I try to say something, but nothing comes out of my mouth.

"Mallory, we were very upset when we heard what happened while we were gone," says Mom.

Dad starts driving and pulls into our driveway. "Let's go inside and get settled and then we'll talk," says Dad.

I follow my parents and their suitcases into the house. I hope it takes them a long time to "get settled," but it doesn't. They put their suitcases down, tell Max hello, and pay Crystal. Then they tell me to go to my room.

For once, I hope I am the only one who is going to my room. But no such luck. My parents follow me in and shut the door. I sit down on my bed. I wait for my parents to sit down too, but they don't.

"Mallory, Mom and I are trying to understand why you would do what you did." Dad shakes his head. "How could you do that to your brother?"

Both of my parents look at me like I'm a stranger and not their daughter.

My throat feels tight. I was upset earlier when Max, Winnie, and Crystal were mad. But this is worse. Mom and Dad are more than just mad. I can tell that they are disappointed in me too. Tears are starting to form in the corners of my eyes. I try to blink them back.

Mom and Dad look at me, waiting for my explanation.

I try to explain things so my parents will understand.

"I wasn't trying to do anything to Max. But ever since Max and Winnie became 'official,' they have been spending a lot of time together and none of it includes me."

I stop for a second to see if that makes sense to Mom and Dad, but they just keep looking at me. I try to explain to my parents that I wouldn't have had to snoop on my brother if had just included me a little bit in what he was doing.

Dad shakes his head again. "Mallory, your brother is growing up. Like it or not, he is entitled to some privacy. You are not allowed to snoop on him."

Now it is my turn to shake my head. "He shouldn't be allowed to leave me out of things."

Dad sits down on the bed beside me. "Mallory, Max has a girlfriend now," says Dad. "It is nice that you want to spend time with him, and I know there are times that he wants to be with you too." Dad looks at me like he really wants me to listen to what he is about to say. "To be honest, Mallory, you seemed to have developed a much stronger interest in being with your brother since he got a girlfriend." Dad pauses. "But there are going to be times when Max and Winnie want to be together. They might not want you to be part of what they're doing. When that's the case, you need to give them their privacy. Do you understand?"

I think about it for a minute. I know that "giving them their privacy" is Dad's way of saying "stay out of their business." The truth is, I don't like the feeling of not knowing what's going on in my brother's life, but I also don't like the feeling of sneaking, peeking, and spying. I know Max was really mad at me, and even though a lot of times he makes me mad, I don't like when he's mad at me. I look at Mom and Dad like what I am about to say is important. "No more snooping," I say to my parents.

My parents seem like they're satisfied that I get that.

"Mallory, I'm glad to hear you're not planning to do any more snooping," says Dad. He gets a very serious look on his face. "But it still doesn't explain why you said things about your brother and Winnie to other people, and particularly things that just weren't true."

I look down at a ball of fuzz on my bedspread. I'm pretty good at thinking up explanations, but I don't have one for this. Now I really feel badly about what I did. Max and Winnie were very upset, and to be honest, I don't blame them. I guess I would be upset too if someone did to me what I did to them.

"I don't know why I did it," I say. "I guess I just wanted everyone to know there was a reason why I was interested in finding out what Max and Winnie were doing when they were together." I take a deep breath.

"I know what I did was wrong."

Mom nods her head to agree.

"You owe your brother an apology," says Dad. "Winnie too."

"I apologized to them yesterday, but neither one of them accepted my apology," I tell my parents. "They're really mad."

Dad makes a weird clicking noise with his mouth like that is too bad but understandable.

Mom makes the same noise like she agrees with Dad.

Instead of making weird clicking noises, I wish my parents would say something helpful like, "Don't worry,

Mallory, we'll help you think of a good way to say you're sorry."

But my parents don't say that. It looks like I'm going to have to think of my own way to say I'm sorry so Max and Winnie accept my apology. I scratch my head. My brother and his girlfriend are seriously mad.

I scratch the side of my head and send a message to my brain.

It is time for my brain to do some very serious thinking.

M.I.A.

It's Sunday morning.

Last night, I set my alarm for 6:30 A.M. But I wake up at 6:27, before it goes off. I hop out of bed, turn off the alarm, and throw on some clothes. I take the sheet of paper from my desk that has this morning's schedule on it. I fold it carefully and slip it into my back pocket.

It's time for me to go *M.I.A.*

I open my window and climb out. It's still kind of dark outside. I don't think I've ever been up this early.

Some people think *M.I.A.* means "missing in action." But in this case, it means "Mallory in Action."

I walk next door and knock on my best friend's window.

Right when I do, she opens it.

"You're up early," I say happily.

"It's the least I can do to help my best friend." Mary Ann grins as she climbs out.

Last night when I called Mary Ann and told her about my plan, she promised she would help me. I've got a lot to do this morning and not much time to do it. I give my best friend a hug. This is one of those times when I really need her.

Mary Ann hugs me back like she really is happy to help me.

"OK. First stop, the kitchen," I say.

"Lead the way," says Mary Ann. She pushes me back toward my window, and we both climb in.

When we get to the kitchen, I pull my schedule out of my back pocket and unfold it. "Step one. Time to bake." I tell Mary Ann.

She opens Mom's cookbook and starts

reading off ingredients.

"Flour."

"Check," I say as I pull it out of a cabinet.

"Sugar. Butter."

I open another cabinet and the refrigerator.

"Check. Check."

"Eggs. Vanilla. Chocolate Chips."

"Check. Check. Check."

When I'm done getting out ingredients, I take out a mixing bowl. Mary Ann and I start stirring and blending. I mix together butter and sugar while she cracks the eggs. We add in the rest of the ingredients. I turn on the oven while Mary Ann drops little balls of dough on a cookie sheet. When the oven is hot, I put the cookie sheet in the oven and set the timer.

"Step two. Time to cut and paste."

And I don't mean the kind of cutting
and pasting you do on the computer.
I mean the kind you do at the kitchen
table with construction paper, glitter,
glue, and markers.

Mary Ann and I sit down. I start cutting
out hearts and Mary Ann cuts stars. When
we're done cutting, Mary Ann glues, while
I glitter. When we finish, I turn over the
schedule that I made last night. On the
back, I already wrote out what I want to
write on the construction paper. I wanted
to make sure I said everything just the
right way, and I knew I couldn't do that if I
was in a rush. I copy what I wrote.

When I'm done, I let out a deep breath.
I'm relieved to be through. Mary Ann reads
what I wrote. "I think they're really going
to like them," she says.

I cross my toes. "I hope they do."

"Of course they will," says Mary Ann. "They'll see that you wanted to do something to show them how badly you feel. And they can't stay mad forever."

Mary Ann and I look at each other. Then we both laugh. We both know the truth, which is that Max won't stay mad forever, but Winnie might. She's not exactly what you would call forgiving.

The buzzer interrupts our laughter. I grab the big oven mitt and take the cookie sheet out of the oven.

While I'm waiting for the cookies to cool, I take out two plates, put a lacy paper doily on each one and pour two glasses of milk.

I lick both envelopes and seal them shut.

"You really think this will work?" I ask Mary Ann.

"Of course!" she says like she is 100% sure that my plan will work.

I give her another hug. She always knows just what to say to me and just how to say it.

She pokes the top of one of the cookies. "They're ready," she says.

I use a spatula and pile cookies on each plate. When I'm done, Mary Ann hands me a card and a glass of milk. "You'd better get going before it's too late."

"Thanks again for your help," I say.

"No problem." Mary Ann turns me around and gives me a little push toward Max's room. "Delivery time," she says.

I look down at the plate I'm holding. I know the cookies are ready. I just hope the delivery girl is.

PEACE, LOVE, AND COOKIES

I pause outside my brother's room.

"Wish me luck," I whisper to Cheeseburger.

She purrs and rubs up against my leg.

I can hear Max already making waking-up noises. It's now or never. Since my hands are full, I tap on Max's door with my foot.

"Who is it?" a sleepy voice asks.

But I don't answer. I don't want Max to tell me not to come in when he finds out who it is. I stack the card and the plate of cookies I'm holding on top of the glass of milk and carefully open Max's door with my free hand.

I can't tell if Max is *first-thing-in-the-morning-grumpy* or just not happy to see me. I take a deep breath and ignore his look. I hope he'll like what I have for him.

"Surprise!" I say to my brother. I walk over to his bed and hand him the plate of cookies and card I made for him. Champ tries to stick his face in the plate, but I push him off the bed.

Max looks confused, so I explain.

"I wanted to do something nice for you," I tell my brother. Max picks up the card.

I wait for him to finish reading before I start talking.

"Max. I want you to know I really am sorry I was a snoop," I say. I look down at the plate and card in Max's hands, and then I keep explaining.

"Part of it was that I wanted to do what you were doing. You're my brother, and I wanted to hang out with you and Winnie."

Max rolls his eyes like that explanation doesn't sound completely true to him. And the truth is . . . it isn't. Max knows I don't usually want to just do what he's doing or hang out with him.

"OK. Part of me did want to do what you were doing. But a bigger part of me wanted to know what you were doing."

Max points to his desk. It's covered in bread. White bread. Wheat bread. Thick bread. Thin bread. Rye bread. French bread. Bagels. Hot dog buns. And even tortillas. I'm not sure how I didn't notice it there when I hid in his closet.

"Winnie and I were working on our science fair project."

Max gets out of bed. He turns around three poster boards stacked against his wall. I read what is written on them. "Do all types of bread mold at the same rate?" I say out loud.

"The answer is no," says Max. "If you look at the project Winnie and I did, you will see that all breads do not mold at the same rate. All breads do not have the same ingredients so they mold at different rates. Also, it depends on the thickness of the bread.

I look down at a spot on my jeans. I feel really bad. "Your project is really good." I pause. "I know I was being an annoying little sister. I'm really sorry, and I promise I won't be one ever again."

"Ever?" Max raises an eyebrow and gives me a look like that's a promise I probably won't be able to keep.

"OK. I'll *try* not to be an annoying little sister," I say.

I wait for Max to laugh or smile or pick up a cookie or even say he's going to make me eat moldy bread if I don't stay out of his business, but he doesn't do any of that. He just looks at me like there's something else I should say, and I know what it is.

"I'm also really sorry I said stuff that wasn't true about you and Winnie. It was wrong and I'm sorry."

Max still doesn't say anything.

Now I don't know what else to say, so I just shrug my shoulders. I've said everything I came to say.

Max sits there for a few minutes, and then he starts talking.

"Mallory, I get that you want to hang out with me some of the time." I can tell Max is thinking carefully about what he wants to say before he says it. "I like hanging out with you some of the time too."

I smile at what Max just said. But he holds up his hand traffic-cop style, like I should hold my smile until he's finished talking.

"The thing is . . . when I'm with Winnie, I don't want to hang out with you. Do you understand what I'm saying?"

I nod.

"Maybe we need a code phrase," I say to Max. "When you're with Winnie and you don't want me to come in your room, you can just say, 'The British are coming!' And I'll know you don't want me to come in." I wink at Max. "It'll be our secret plan."

But Max shakes his head. "We don't need a secret plan. Just leave me alone when I'm with Winnie. Get it?"

I look down. "Got it," I say. I probably should have gotten it earlier. Mom and Dad and Crystal have already explained it to me. Max is growing up, and I have to give him some privacy. Part of me doesn't like it, but I get it.

"And Mallory, you can't just go around

saying stuff about other people, especially when it's not true."

"I know." And I really do know. "Max, I really am sorry. I promise I won't spread any rumors about you or Winnie or anybody else."

Max looks at me like there's more I should be promising.

I think I know what he wants. I raise my right hand. "I promise never to snoop again."

"OK," Max says like he's satisfied with my answer. He smiles and picks up a cookie. I watch while he shoves it into his mouth and listen while he makes a bunch of *I'm-really-liking-what-I'm-eating* noises.

"Wow! Those are amazing!" Max grins and then picks up another cookie, shoves it into his mouth, and washes it down with a glass of milk.

Now it's my turn to grin. "I'm glad you

like them. I wanted to do something you would like." Then I stop grinning. "There's someone else I want to do something nice for, and I want to do it before she gets out of bed." I tell Max that I'm taking cookies and a card next door to Winnie.

"Hmmm." Max makes a noise like that's an interesting idea, but not necessarily a good one.

"Do you think Winnie will forgive me?" I ask Max. "I know she was pretty upset about some of the things I said."

Max gives me a serious look. "She was mad, and when Winnie is mad, it's hard to get her un-mad. Believe me, I know."

Max and I look at each other. Then we both start laughing, like we're both on the same team on this one.

"Good luck," Max says.

"I think I'll need it," I say.

When I say that, we laugh even harder, and once we start, we can't stop.

I don't know why we're laughing so hard. I don't really know what was so funny. But what I do know is that it feels really good to be laughing with my brother.

I really hope Winnie likes the cookies and that she'll accept my apology, but even if she doesn't, the person that matters most to me already did.

A RECIPE

Have you ever heard the expression "waking up on the wrong side of the bed?" It means to wake up in a grumpy mood, and it happens all the time.

I have a sure cure to get people (my brother and believe it or not, Winnie) un-grumpy. Just give them a sincere apology and double chocolate chip cookies first thing in the morning. In case you need to get someone un-grumpy, I'm giving you my special recipe.

Double Chocolate Chip Cookies
Recipe by Mallory McDonald

Cream together:
2 sticks butter
¾ cup white sugar
¾ cup brown sugar

Add:

2 eggs

2 teaspoons vanilla

Combine and mix in:

2¼ cups flour

½ teaspoon salt

1 teaspoon baking soda

Stir in:

1 12 oz. bag semisweet chocolate chips

1 12 oz. bag milk chocolate chips

1 cup of chopped pecans (if you like nuts)

Spoon dough onto nonstick cookie sheets. Heat oven to 375 degrees. Bake 11 minutes. Cool on racks. Put on a plate and serve to grumpy people. Watch them smile!

And in case you're looking for a recipe to make sure your parents come home from a trip happy, I have a recipe for that too.

All you have to do is make sure you don't do anything while they're gone that will make them unhappy. Trust me when I tell you, this recipe works every time.

I hope you like my recipes!

A PLEDGE

Even though I made cookies (really delicious ones) and apologized to Max this morning, I could tell he still didn't believe me that I was going to stop snooping. So this afternoon, I made a pinky swear with him that I would never do it again.

But when we were done, Max gave me a *does-a-pinky-swear-really-mean-anything?* look. So I gave Max more than a pinky swear.

I gave him a pledge, and it went like this:

A Pledge
By Mallory McDonald

I pledge allegiance to the flag of the United States of Max, and to the republic for which it stands, one nation under Max, indivisible, with liberty and justice for all that I will never snoop again.

When I finished pledging, Max shook his head and looked at me like I was crazy. He told me that pledge made absolutely no sense and that all this baking and pinky-swearing and pledging wasn't really necessary. He said the only thing he really wanted was for me to just leave him alone when he's busy with other people.

I winked and asked him if he meant certain people in particular.

Max rolled his eyes like I was being annoying. So I double, triple promised to do that. Then I handed him the flag I made and told him he could keep it.

Max stuck it on top of his bedpost and we both watched it flap in the air-conditioning.

Then he looked down and smiled at me. I think things at 17 Wish Pond Road are back to normal. At least for now.

PLAYING GAMES

If you're looking for something fun to do with your friends, it's always fun to play games. Hide-and-Seek is one of my favorites. I don't think you should try playing it the way I played it, but there are lots of fun ways you can play.

Way #1: Hide-and-seek One person is "it." Everyone else hides. "It" counts to one-hundred and then starts looking. The first person found becomes "it" for the next round. "It" keeps looking until everyone is found. Usually no one gets a prize, but everyone agrees that the last person found had the best hiding place. If the person who is "it" gives up looking before everyone is found, he or she just yells something like, "Come out, come out, wherever you are!" and that round is over.

Way #2: Sardines

The first time I played this was last summer at camp. It's really fun. One person hides. Everyone else counts, then starts looking for the person who is hiding. When each person finds the person who is hiding, he or she hides with that person. The last person to find the group that's hiding is the loser and has to hide in the next round.

Way #3: Midnight

This game is just like hide-and-seek, but you play it outside at night. Whoever is "it" starts counting out loud the time on the clock up to midnight (one o'clock, two o'clock, and so on) while everyone else hides outside. The person who is "it" shouts out "midnight" and starts looking for everyone. It's really fun to be "it" in this game, because you get to use a flashlight to look for everyone.

Way #4: Bloody Murder

This is my favorite way to play. It's kind of like playing tag but with a scary, cool name. One person hides while everyone else counts and then looks. When someone finds the person who is hiding, he or she shouts out "Bloody Murder!" Then it becomes a game of tag, with the hider as "it." Everyone has to run to a home base, and the last person that "it" tags becomes the person who hides in the next round.

If you don't like any of these ways, you can make up your own way to play. Whatever games you decide to play, I hope you have lots and lots and lots of fun playing them!

Talk to you soon!

Big, huge hugs and kisses!

Mallory

Carolrhoda Books
A division of Lerner Publishing Group, Inc.
241 First Avenue North
Minneapolis, MN 55401 U.S.A.

Website address: www.lernerbooks.com

cover background © iStockphoto.com/Yahya Idiz

SUSTAINABLE
FORESTRY
INITIATIVE

Certified Chain of Custody
Promoting Sustainable Forestry
www.sfiprogram.org
SFI-01268

SFI label applies to the text stock

Library of Congress Cataloging-in-Publication Data

Friedman, Laurie
    Mallory McDonald, super snoop / by Laurie Friedman ; illustrations by
Jennifer Kalis.
        p.   cm. — (Mallory ; #18)
    Summary: Ten-year-old Mallory, determined to find out what her
brother, Max, does while spending time with his girlfriend, Winnie, spies
an innocent kiss on the cheek, then tells her babysitter and friends a
more exciting tale. Includes a recipe for double chocolate chip cookies and
directions for playing four games.
        ISBN: 978-0-7613-6073-5 (trade hardcover : alk. paper)
        ISBN: 978-1-4677-0031-3 (eBook)
        [1. Brothers and sisters—Fiction. 2. Dating (Social customs)—Fiction.
3. Gossip—Fiction. 4. Babysitters—Fiction. 5. Family life—Fiction.] I. Kalis,
Jennifer, ill. II. Title.
PZ7.F89773Mahm 2012
[Fic]—dc23   2011044332

Manufactured in the United States of America
2 — BP — 7/1/13